Rockets

CROOK CATCHERS

The Stuff-It-In Specials

Karen Wallace &
Judy Brown

Rockets

CROOK CATCHERS

Karen Wallace & Judy Brown

The Stuff-it-in Specials
The Minestrone Mob
The Sandwich Scam
The Peanut Prankster

First paperback edition 2000
First published 1999 in hardback by
A & C Black (Publishers) Ltd
35 Bedford Row, London WC1R 4JH

ISBN 0-7136-5129-6

A CIP catalogue record for this book is available
from the British Library.

Printed and bound by G. Z. Printek, Bilbao, Spain.

Chapter One

Lettuce Leef and Nimble Charlie were
Crook Catchers to the Queen.
They believed in three things.

And today the Queen had asked the
Crook Catchers to lunch...

Lettuce Leef and Nimble Charlie headed off to the Palace. Usually the Queen's guards marched round and round the courtyard or else stood very still in front of the gates.

But today they were doing all sorts of
silly things. Some were even standing on
each other's shoulders and jumping over
the wall into the street.

5

'Beserko battalions!' cried Nimble Charlie.

Lettuce Leef ran across the courtyard.

Chapter Two

The Queen stood in the doorway.

Lettuce Leef bowed.

Nimble Charlie curtseyed. But only because he was nervous.

'Your Majesty,' cried Lettuce Leef.

'We don't look at anything except our plate at lunchtime,' cried the Queen. She smacked her lips and rang a bell.

Splatter, the Queen's
trusty servant,
raced into the
room with a trolley.

He grabbed the top off a silver dish and
did a backwards somersault.

Something very peculiar lay on the silver dish. It was warm and gooey.

It was round and lumpy.

It had sticky green bits in it.

Splatter grinned a silly grin. 'Stanley
Slob made it especially for you!'

'Who is Stanley Slob?' Lettuce Leef asked Splatter.

Splatter twirled in a circle and put a lampshade over his head.

Lettuce Leef looked serious.

At that moment, a huge crash came from outside. Everyone jumped up and looked out of the window.

The guards were playing pick-a-stick with their swords!

'This is outrageous,' cried the Queen.

'Stanley Slob wants everyone to be silly just like him,' giggled Splatter.

Chapter Three

Ten minutes later, the prime
minister bounced through the door.

The Queen clenched her teeth.

The prime minister switched on the
television and pointed at the screen.

Lettuce Leef and Nimble Charlie gasped.
Teachers were ripping up books.

Bank managers were throwing money
into the streets.

Suddenly a fat, spotty face appeared
on the screen.

The Queen went purple with rage.

The Queen turned and glared at the
prime minister.

The prime minister poured a
bucket of custard over his head and
bounced out of the room.

The Queen fell into her armchair and stared at the thing on the dish.

'Don't worry, Your Majesty,' said Lettuce Leef. 'We'll stop Stanley Slob.'

Chapter Four

Nimble Charlie and Lettuce Leef raced back to their pumpkin office.

Lettuce Leef bit into a carrot.

Suddenly there was a knock at the door.

Nimble Charlie opened the door.

The postman giggled.

Everyone's got one!

He dumped a parcel on the table and back-flipped to his van.

Lettuce Leef and Nimble Charlie stared at the parcel. It was wrapped in yellow paper tied with a slime-green ribbon.

Lettuce Leef examined the parcel but found nothing.

Nimble Charlie sniffed the parcel.
It smelt sweet and greasy and stale.

'I bet Stanley Slob wrapped this himself,'
he said. Lettuce Leef stared at the parcel.

She picked up the telephone and tapped
out a number. 'Hello, Dial-a-Dog?'

Chapter Five

Bob the bloodhound was the best sniffer dog in the business.

He took one sniff of the parcel and ran out the door howling.

Lettuce Leef didn't know what to do.

A minute later Lettuce Leef and
Nimble Charlie sped off down the
street after Bob.

Bob the bloodhound sniffed round corner shops.

He snuffled in big department stores.

His nose twitched at little food stands.

Suddenly Bob screeched to a halt at
a crossroads.

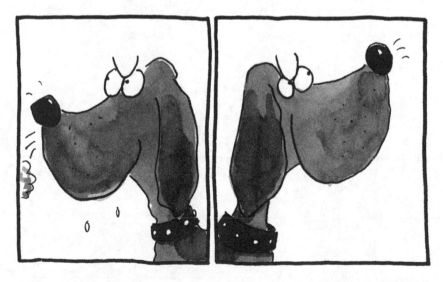

He sniffed left.   He sniffed right.

He sniffed at the
bottom of a
metal ladder
that went up
the side
of a huge
warehouse.

Then he
let out an
enormous
howl!

'Looks like we've found Stanley Slob!'
said Lettuce Leef. She stared at a
letter box painted to look like a
Stuff-it-in Special.

'And his factory,' said Nimble
Charlie, holding his nose.

So how are we going to catch him?

Lettuce Leef took a big envelope out of her pocket and pushed it through the letter box.

The next morning Stanley Slob
jumped out of bed.

He ran downstairs and ripped open
the envelope!

Boilingham Palace

Queen requires
genius to help
rule the country.
Only Stanley
Slob need apply

signed The Queen

Stanley Slob held up the hand-mirror that hung from his belt. 'Who's a clever boy?' he murmured.

Chapter Six

Back at the pumpkin office, Lettuce Leef and Nimble Charlie had just finished breakfast when the Queen burst in.

'Excellent!' cried Lettuce Leef.
'My plan has worked!'
She grabbed a huge net.

The Queen gave an ear-splitting whistle.

Two minutes later they raced into the Palace garden. Twenty corgis charged after them. Each one was holding the edge of a large, round net.

Sure enough, there was Stanley Slob
holding a Stuff-it-in Special.

Stanley Slob was amazed! This wasn't
what he was expecting at all!

He dropped the Stuff-it-in Special...

...ran through
a flower bed...

...and into the
vegetable
garden.

'You won't catch me!' he squealed.

Phew!

But Stanley Slob had eaten too many
Stuff-it-in Specials!
He couldn't run fast at all!
Puffing like a steam train, he tried
to hide in the Queen's cabbages.

Too late!
The net was over his head before you
could say chopped carrots!

'You are a very bad boy,' said the Queen.
'What are you?'

The Queen waggled her finger.

She turned to Lettuce Leef and
Nimble Charlie.

45

Stanley Slob crawled from under the net.
Suddenly Lettuce Leef felt sorry for him.

'Put him on a diet,' she said to the Queen.

The Queen was so pleased Stanley Slob
had been captured she did a backwards
somersault without even thinking!

Lettuce Leef winked at Nimble Charlie
and bit into a carrot.

The End